THAT PESKY PICKLE

Story by Jamie Cannon
Illustrated by Gene Schrader

For D, a genius of a boy who lights up every corner of my world and inspired this book.

Thank you for always being you and showing me the real way to be brave.

Copyright ©2019 Jamie Cannon, All Rights Reserved.

No part of this publication may be reproduced, distributed, or transmitted in any form or by any means, including photocopying, recording, or other electronic or mechanical methods, without the prior written permission of the author, except in the case of brief quotations embodied in reviews and certain other non-commercial uses permitted by copyright law.

ISBN #9780578575506

THAT PESKY PICKLE

Story by Jamie Cannon • Illustrated by Gene Schrader

It all started when that pesky pickle stayed out after dark.

"Don't get lost" his mama warned.

He got lost.

"Not to worry" he declared. "Pickles aren't afraid of the dark."

So that brave, pesky pickle hitched up his socks
and ventured off.

Things started off pretty good.

He took a spin on a trolley car that zoomed through the streets,

and the bakery on the corner gave him their "end of the night pink sprinkled special."

Then IT happened.

He ran into an absolute, real-as-can-be monster.

The kind that scares the socks right off you.

Pickles may not be afraid of the dark,
but there is one for sure thing that terrifies them.

MONSTERS.

The minute that pesky pickle felt the WHOOSH of air from the monster's long crinkly arm, he did what any brave pickle would do.

He RAN.

Without a single thought, he shot away from that monster and caught the closest trolley out of there.

Once he was safe, that pesky pickle started to notice his tummy hurting.

He had never been ALONE with a monster before!

After about 7 blocks, that poor pesky pickle calmed down enough to sneak a look behind him—which was a terrible, horrible idea.

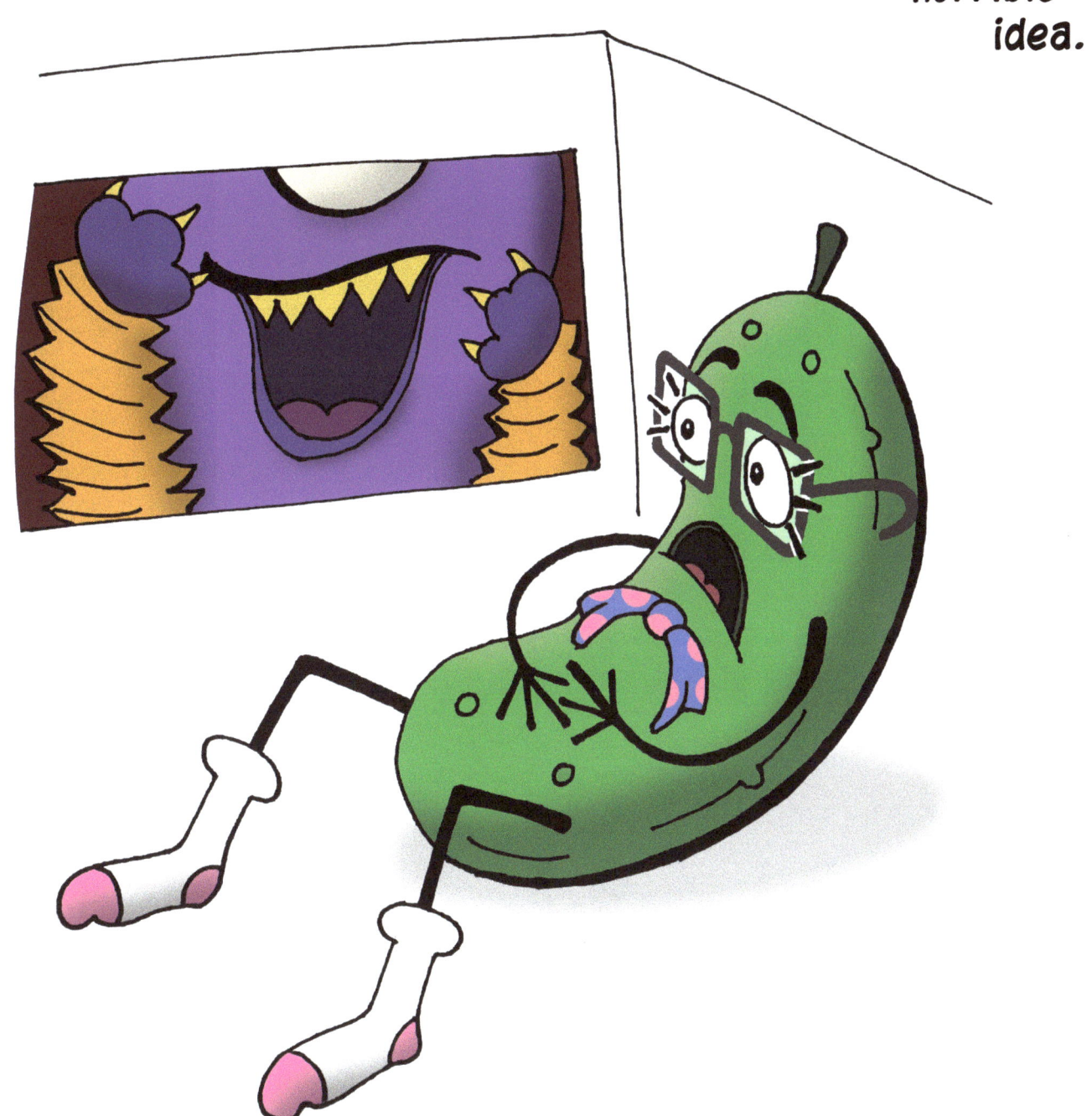

Peeking outside, he spied those crinkly monster arms and hole-of-a-mouth still following him!

That brave, pesky pickle panicked. He barreled sideways
off the trolley and tumbled down a hill,
soaring sky high into the air

Into someone's garden of cabbages.

The minute he landed, that pesky pickle started to cry.

He cried so hard and so long, his glasses almost washed right off his face.

"I'm so far from home, with that frightful thing chasing me. I will never ever make it back again!!"

That poor pesky pickle started to think about his warm house and his Mama's cookies.

He started to miss his home so much, it made his insides hurt.

"Maybe I am not that brave" he whispered to himself.

Suddenly, that pesky pickle could feel someone watching him. He jumped up, ready to run, and came face to face with...

"a cabbage?"

"At your service, sir!"

"It sounded like you could really use some help."

That pesky pickle stood still as a statue, feeling rather embarrassed.

"Well, you see...I was exploring, and it may have gotten dark sooner than I expected. And...well, I may have encountered something very unusual after it got dark...and..."

"No need to say anymore, sir. I understand. Sometimes the dark can play tricks on us."

That pesky pickle felt relieved. "You sound like someone I can really depend on."

"Pleased to meet you sir. You can call me Maverick."

"So, what is our mission sir? Sounded like there's an enemy around here?"

That pesky pickle sighed. "Can I tell you something? I have discovered I don't like being alone in the dark and would like to find my way back home."

Maverick took that pesky pickle's hand and nodded. "Understood, sir. Count on me to help."

That pesky pickle and Maverick started off together, into the shadows.

They walked so far in the dark, their legs started wobbling. No matter how hard he stared, nothing looked familiar to that pesky pickle.

He couldn't figure out how he managed to get so far from home!

Maverick had an idea. "What if you think back to where you started? That might give us a clue."

That pesky pickle stopped and pondered. He remembered that he started off brave and ready to go on an adventure. He remembered that he met some new people and tried new things.

(He skipped over remembering the part about that THING.)

Then, it came to him. Suddenly he remembered that right before he ran into that terrible, horrible monster he was walking through a park that had just closed.

"I've got it!" he yelled. He was so excited he started to hiccup.

"I just need to go backwards until I find that park! I got so distracted by that dreadful monster I ran the complete wrong direction!"

That pesky pickle took off at top pickle speed back through the gloomy streets, cabbage in tow.

"C'mon Maverick!" he shrieked. "It's all coming back to me!"

And sure enough, that pesky pickle managed to drag that little cabbage through blocks of darkness until they popped out into an enormous park.

"This is it!"

They stood for a minute, catching their breath. Maverick thought that pesky pickle was the bravest thing he had ever seen.

"Sir, you are amazing. Never have I ever seen someone so afraid turn around and find their way out like you just did."

That pesky pickle looked delighted.
"Thank you, Maverick. You helped me remember what was important, and that helped me get home."

Maverick nodded.
"Well, sir, you go ahead and head home then. I'm going to rest my legs here a bit, then head back to my home too."

That pesky pickle scooped Maverick up in an enormous pickle hug. "Thank you, Maverick. You are a true blue friend."

After he said goodbye, that pesky pickle headed off.

On his way out of the park, he noticed something crinkly out of the corner of his eye and jumped.

"It cannot be!" he muttered.
But there it was, that horrible, terrible monster...

hanging right in front of him on a...

"balloon cart?"

That pesky pickle could not believe his eyes.

His monster was a balloon!! This whole time, that frightful thing chasing him was nothing more than a lonely little balloon that someone had left at the park.

He laughed until his glasses were crooked.

"It must have wanted to be with me" he announced. "That poor baby balloon was looking for his mama the whole time, too!"

That pesky pickle tied that cute little balloon onto his wrist and thought how odd it was that he wasn't afraid anymore.

"Pickles really are the bravest things" he whispered on his way home.

CPSIA information can be obtained
at www.ICGtesting.com
Printed in the USA
BVHW091155211021
619528BV00005B/170